A TRUE STORY ABOUT JACKIE ROBINSON

Testing the Ice

BY

SHARON ROBINSON

ILLUSTRATED BY

KADIR NELSON

SCHOLASTIC PRESS / NEW YORK

The year was 1955.

Dad was in his ninth season with

the Brooklyn Dodgers, and for the

third time in four years, they faced

the New York Yankees in the

World Series!

When my father stole home

in the first game, Yogi Berra,

the Yankee catcher, screamed,

"He's out!"

The umpire, however, shouted,

"He's safe!"

It took seven games, but the

Brooklyn Dodgers finally beat

the New York Yankees!

Oh, how we celebrated!

Earlier that same year, my family moved

from Queens in New York City to Cascade Road in Stamford,

Connecticut. Our new house sat in the middle of six acres on a

narrow, twisted road named for the waterfall at the end of it.

The best part, according to my father, was the woods

on three sides of the house, which screened us from passing

cars and curious strangers.

But to my brothers, Jackie Jr. and David, and me,

the best parts were our new friends Candy, Willie,

and Christy—and the lake that ran from our yard

to our neighbor's yard, a whole quarter mile away.

We spent our first summer playing by the lake.

We had picnics, we swam, and we rowed our

boats. But no matter how much we begged,

my dad would *never* come into the water.

How our friends loved playing inside our house!

Our playroom had a pool table, a soda fountain—and

a huge gray boulder that was built into the wall! And

while we took it all for granted, our friends made a big

fuss over Dad's trophy room. They stared adoringly

at his plaques, his silver bat, the signed baseballs, and

Dad's bronzed college football cleat. And they asked

him questions in ways we never thought

to ask. Then, one rainy Saturday morning

over a game of Monopoly, they got Dad

talking about his historic entry into Major

League Baseball.

"Baseball, like most of America, was segregated," Dad began. "Major League Baseball was for whites only. Black- and brown-skinned players had to play in the Negro Leagues. Some of the greatest baseball players were not white. They were denied entry into the major leagues—just because of the color of their skin.

"Finding food worth eating or a restaurant to serve us was a daily problem. In many places we played, there was no hotel that allowed blacks. That was just the way things were in 1945, and no one expected them to change.

"I was playing for the Monarchs when Branch Rickey approached me. He told me he could get me into the Brooklyn Dodgers!

"'I know you're a good ballplayer,' Mr. Rickey barked. 'But do you have the guts for this?'

"The next few minutes were tough as Rickey warned that I would be called all kinds of names, threatened, and attacked physically. The next question he asked startled me even more: Could I take all of this and still control my temper?

"I thought of the doors opening to other black players after me, and how the color barrier of baseball would be shattered. There was only one answer.

"'I'll do it!' I said.

"Playing that first spring was tough—especially the game between the Dodgers and the Phillies. Some fans cheered me. Others shouted insults that were so bad I had to struggle to keep my temper from exploding.

"After seven scoreless innings, we got the Phillies out in the eighth and it was our turn at bat. I led off. The insults were still coming. I lined into center field for a single, then took my lead. I cut out for second. The Phillies pitcher threw wide. The ball bounced past the shortstop. I rounded third and made it home.

"That was a sweet victory."

We all sat there wide-eyed, listening to his every word.

My dad was amazing.

"Guess you showed Mr. Rickey that you had guts!" Candy said.

"Sure did," Jackie Jr. replied proudly. "That's why he won the first Rookie of the Year award."

"Yeah, and the Most Valuable Player award, too," Willie added. "Bet you'll even get into the Hall of Fame someday!"

Dad wasn't much into bragging, but I caught his lips curl into a smile.

Dad retired after the 1956 season in a surprise move that shocked

his fans. But he didn't stop there. . . .

After baseball, Dad took a job as vice president of a popular

coffee company, wrote books, walked in protest marches

alongside Dr. Martin Luther King, Jr., and raised

money for the Civil Rights Movement.

And best of all, he was home more.

With Dad home, we did more as a family. The

lake provided us with the most fun through every

season of the year. In the spring, we watched frog

eggs hatch into tadpoles.

We fished, rowed the boat to sandbanks, and captured turtles

napping in the sun. But Dad stayed dry on the shoreline.

In the summer, we challenged ourselves to swim across the width

of the lake. But Dad cheered from the safety of the sandy shore.

No matter how hard we pressed, Dad always found a reason

not to get into the water.

In the winter, the lake froze. My brothers and I huddled in the

living room with our parents as we listened to the eerie sounds it

made. It howled and moaned throughout the night. As the ice

thickened, the sounds deepened. We waited nearly a week before

popping the big question.

We found Dad sitting by the fireplace, reading the newspaper.
A hot fire crackled and hissed.

"We want to go ice-skating!" we all shouted together.

He looked up into six eager faces. "What did your mother say?"

"She said we could," we told him. "Just as long as you come
with us."

Dad looked anxious. "It's below freezing!" he reminded us.

"Then the ice should be good and frozen," Jackie Jr. said.

"Yeah, strong enough to hold even you," David chimed in.

"Please, Mr. Robinson," Candy and Willie pleaded together.
"Christy and I want to practice making figure eights," I added.
Dad smiled proudly. "So it's figure eights today, is it, Shar?"
I beamed. "Yes, Daddy. We've been practicing in our socks."
"Well, in that case," he said, hiding sheepishly behind his
newspaper, "I guess we should go."

The mad scramble began. We all ran from room to room looking for Dad's gloves, hat, and coat. Then we stood in front of Dad's chair, pleading, making funny faces and hurry-up hand signs until he finally put down the paper. Very slowly, he pulled on one giant black rubber boot, then the other.

When Dad was dressed, he reluctantly led the way. We marched behind him, pushing him as we walked out the sliding glass doors,

When we reached the edge of the lake, Dad turned to us and

said, "Wait!" Jackie, David, Candy, Willie, Christy, and I

came to an abrupt halt. Then he ran to the house and returned

with a shovel and a broomstick.

As we lined up along the lake's edge, Dad eased onto the

snow-covered ice.

"Dad, be careful!" I shouted.

"Don't fall in!" David screamed.

I grabbed Christy's mittened hand and squeezed.

"What's wrong?" she whispered.

"I'm scared," I replied, as the reality suddenly dawned on me. "My dad can't swim."

Jackie Jr. twisted the cord attached to his sled.

David, Candy, and Willie stepped closer to the edge of the lake.

Dad went farther out. The ice crackled beneath his feet. He took another step, then cleared the snow from his path with the shovel. From the cleared spot he was able to tell how thick the ice was. Before he placed one big foot in front of the other, he tapped the ice with his broomstick, testing it for weaknesses or cracks.

Tap, tap, tap. Dad took a few steps forward.

Tap, tap, tap. Then he took a few more steps.

But just as he was about to pronounce the ice safe—

B O O O O O M !

A terrible noise roared from below the ice.

"Dad!" I shrieked. I was sure the ice was going to open up and swallow him!

Jackie Jr. stood ready to shove his sled to Dad. David, Candy, and Willie inched closer to my brother.

We waited for what seemed like forever.

"It was just an air bubble!" Dad called

to us, as the sound moved down the lake.

Dad took a few more steps, tapping as he moved to

the deepest part of the lake. He stopped, gave one last

tap with his stick, then turned to us and called out,

"It's safe! Put on your skates!"

We cheered as loudly as we could, and we skated circles around

Dad as he walked back onto solid ground. All I could think was:

My dad is the bravest man alive.

Now, years have passed, and we

understand even more how much courage it took for

my father to step out on that ice. In fact, Dad showed

the same courage on the ice that day as he did when he

broke the color barrier in baseball. No one really knew

what would happen. But he felt his way along an untried

path—like a blind man tapping for clues.

That was Jackie Robinson. And that was my dad.

Big, heavy, out there alone on the lake, testing the ice

to be sure it would be safe for us.

And he did it—even though he couldn't swim!

AUTHOR'S NOTE

Until April 15, 1947, Major League Baseball, like much of America, was racially segregated. In baseball, there were no "Jim Crow" laws dictating behavior and supporting the supremacy of one race over another. Instead, there were team owners who set policies and kept blacks and whites playing baseball in separate leagues.

In 1945, Branch Rickey, president of the Brooklyn Dodgers, decided to break the color barrier. This was before President Truman integrated the military, and seven years before the desegregation of schools. After a major search, Mr. Rickey selected Jackie Robinson to pioneer this effort. Robinson was a college-educated man who had lettered in four sports at UCLA—football, baseball, basketball, and track and field—and had played one season with the Negro League team the Kansas City Monarchs.

When Jack Roosevelt Robinson stepped onto the grass of Ebbets Field dressed in Dodger blue, the rule was broken. It was his extraordinary performance and undaunting spirit, in spite of physical and verbal abuse, that kept the doors open. It took thirteen long seasons, but eventually every team had at least one black player on its roster. In those thirteen years, the former Negro Leaguers made an indelible mark on baseball—accounting for six Rookie of the Year awards, nine MVP awards, five home run titles, four batting titles, and a Cy Young Award for Don Newcombe in 1956.

Today, Major League Baseball is reflective of the diverse world we live in. There are still many challenges, like how to get and keep urban kids playing the game and how to rebuild the numbers of African Americans in the majors. But as history has taught us, the struggle for justice and equality is ongoing.

With much love to David Robinson and Jesse Simms—S. R.

For my three rascals: Amel, Aya, and Ali—K. N.

LIBRARY OF CONGRESS CATALOGING-IN-PUBLICATION DATA

Robinson, Sharon, 1950–

Testing the ice : a true story about Jackie Robinson / by Sharon Robinson ; illustrated by Kadir Nelson.—1st ed.   p.   cm.

Summary: As a testament to his courage, Jackie Robinson's daughter shares memories of him, from his baseball career to the day he tests the ice for her, her brothers, and their friends.

ISBN 978-0-545-05251-1 (hardcover) 1. Robinson, Jackie, 1919–1972—Juvenile fiction. [1. Robinson, Jackie, 1919–1972—Fiction. 2. Courage—Fiction. 3. African Americans—Fiction. 4. Baseball—Fiction.]

I. Nelson, Kadir, ill. II. Title. PZ7.R567683Te 2009 [Fic]—dc22 2008038838

10 9 8 7 6 5 4 3 2   10 11 12 13

Printed in Singapore 46   First edition, October 2009

The display type was set in P22 Hopper Josephine. The text was set in Cochin Medium.

The art was created using pencil, watercolor, and oil. Book design by Marijka Kostiw